AF431901

For matters of military secrecy and operational security for the special operations members, most details won't be mentioned in this book.

This book is a work of fiction. Names, characters, places, and incidet either are the product of the author's imagination or, if real, used fictitiously.

Stevie Randall's US Marine Training

Rick Ryan

<u>Weapons depicted</u>

SIG-Sauer P320 Compact/M18

Colt M4A1 assault rifle

Glock 17 pistol

<u>Prologue</u>

One month after she finished her training as part of the US Marine Corps Force Reconnaissance, Stevie Randall was now a member of this very exclusive elite force. And she would be part of an elite reconnaissance team whose job was to infiltrate enemy lines, gather intelligence and transfer said documents to high command. But said mission would also slowly destroy Stevie's innocence.

But for the moment, Stevie had more immediate problems to deal with, since she was going to meet her new squad, which was part of the US Recon Marines, the elite of the US Marine Corps.

Speaking of her squad, it was made up of the commander, 1st Lieutenant Andrew 'AK' Kelley, Sergeant Mike 'Mix' Lopez,

Corporal Dan 'Marky' Marks, Corporal Ted 'Teddy' Hanson and Corporal Drew 'Ecks' Eckins.

Just as she was walking towards her squad, Stevie saw them looking at her in an unamicable way, since the long-serving US Marines always looked down on the rookies, to whom they always had to explain everything from basic battlefield procedures to the most obvious things to do.

But before she could say a word, AK spoke up and said, "Welcome aboard, rookie. Name's AK. Meet the sharpshooter Marky and his spotter Ecks, the tech-guy Teddy and the deputy Mix. You Stevie Randall, right?"

Stevie then replied, "Yes. Why?"

"Well, we'll call you shake. Cause you shake the organization of the squad. Oh, and one rule: you're no use to us dead." Ecks explained to her.

With that said, Stevie, now known as Shake, joined her platoon and attached a silencer, a Trijicon VCOG scope, an AN/PEQ-15 laser sight and a bipod to her M4A1 rifle, since everyone in the squad had these accessories attached to their own M4A1 rifle as well.

The young female US Recon Marine therefore understood the first days of her being part of a recon team was going to be hard. Not knowing her first mission was going to be even harder than in war movies featuring either the US Navy SEALs or the US Recon Marines.

<u>Chapter 1</u>

Two weeks after joining the squad, Shake and her fellow US Marines were embedded alongside the British Royal Marines on the HMS Albion in the Mediterranean Sea en route to the Gulf of Aden. There, the team and a team of British Royal Marines would be tasked with performing a very dangerous mission, consisting to rescue a group of hostages who was being held by the Houthis forces backed by Iran, China and Russia in Yemen. Said hostages were to be rescued alive, since they had information about war crimes perpetrated in Yemen and Ukraine by both the Russians, Chinese and their allies.

And Shake and her team, alongside their British counterparts and allies were preparing their equipment and weapons. Shake remarked that the Royal Marines were using Glock 17 pistols instead of the SIG-Sauer

M18 pistol, even if the British were using the same M4A1 carbine as the team.

Suddenly, Shake began humming a patriotic song before singing it aloud.

"Over there! Over there! - Send the word, send the word - That the Yanks are coming! The Yanks are coming - The drum rum-tumming everywhere! - Over there! Over there! - Send the word, send the word to beware - We'll be over, we're coming over - And we won't come back 'till it's over, over there!"

The US Marine team and the rest of the company then sang *Over There* alongside Shake, as did the British Royal Marines while they all prepared for the mission briefing. And speaking of the briefing, the officer in charge of the mission came to the joint USMC-RM team and motioned them to follow them to the briefing room of the ship.

Once inside the briefing room, the six US Marines and six Royal Marines sat on a set of chairs before a British colonel in his early 50s and a US Major in his late 40s started the briefing.

The USMC Major said, "Welcome everyone. This is going to be your first mission in Yemen. We have located a group of relief workers who are being kept by extremist Houthis helped by Russian Spetsnaz, so do expect some fierce resistance. I'll let over to my British colleague to keep on."

The Royal Marine Colonel announced, "Thank you Major. Your mission consists in rescuing and evacuating five relief workers being held hostage in an unoccupied building in eastern Yemen. Satellite imagery confirms the building has two entry points, one of which is barricaded, and is heavily guarded by at least twenty tangos armed with AK rifles and FAL rifles, plus at least five or ten Spetsnaz armed with AS Val rifles, so expect fierce resistance from them. We can also confirm the hostiles have access to the hostages' laptop, so retrieve it as well. We will drop you at four kilometres from the target at night so that you may operate discreetly behind hostile lines. The five hostages are British national Mark Dugan, Irish national Dan Finnegan, American national Carlos Miller and their two Ukrainian bodyguards. Any question?"

Shake then asked, "Why us? Why not a joint SAS-Navy SEAL-Irish Ranger Wing operation?"

The USMC Major replied, "Because we're the nearest in terms of distance and in terms of reactivity. Did I answer your question?"

"Yes, Sir." Shake replied.

With that, the team was promptly dismissed and went to armory where they retrieved their equipment, weapons and hardware necessary for the raid to be possible at night. Shake and the other participants in the raid knew the

Spetsnaz advisors to the Houthis could likely have night vision goggles, too. Sot they took this factor into account while taking their gear up for the raid.

Meanwhile, in Yemen, the hostages named Mark Dugan, Dan Finnegan, Carlos Miller and their Ukrainian bodyguards were still under the threat of AK rifles wielded by Houthis extremists when a Russian officer wearing his distinctive Gorka suit came in the room where they were detained and ordered the lead militants to prepare his guys to be relieved by the nine other Spetsnaz guys with the officer. The lead militant nodded before saying something in Arabic while the Russian officer said something in Russian to the hostages before spitting at them and whisping them with his MP443 Grach handgun. The Russian then left the room alongside the lead militant.

The Spetsnaz operatives and the Houthi militants then laughed, since they were actually planning to perform a mock execution of the hostages on a video before posting it on social media sites. But little did they know their sinister project for propaganda would never come to fruition.

Indeed, as the hostages in Yemen were being taunted by the sadistic Houthis and Russian Spetsnaz, the rescuers had already finished loading up and were climbing into a British EH101 Merlin helicopter escorted by AW159 gunships armed with Browning M2A1 machine guns.

Inside the EH101, Shake and the others checked their weapons, which were already loaded with full magazines before switching the safety off and putting their weapons in a low ready position. Just then, the ramp gunner motioned the strike team to get ready for landing since the helicopters were seconds away from the landing zone. Shake and the commandos then put their night vision goggles on their eyes before turning the laser module off and putting their shemagh on their face and tore their national insignias off so that no one would be able to identify them as either British or American commandos.

The operation was a high-stake rescue operation which was planned to have the commandos inserted four kilometers away from their target, rescue the hostages and get back to another landing zone. If landing zone was compromised, the commandos were to walk with the hostages to the coast, where rigid-hull boats were going to extract them.

As soon as the commandos jumped off the EH101 Merlin helicopter, the British Royal Marine leader, an Afro-British man named CK, motioned the helicopter and its escort gunship to ward off, which the two birds did. This done, the team and their British allies began walking towards the compound where the hostages were being held by the Houthi militants and their Russian advisors.

Shake, AK, Mix Marky, Ecks, Teddy, CK and their companions walked towards the compound before stopping at around 900 meters away from the target, giving themselves time to observe the enemy and his routine work. Shake took her binoculars and looked through it. She saw the Houthi guards were numbered around 20 with around 10 Spetsnaz operatives walking around and minding their business while porting their AKs and AS Val rifles.

Shake and the rest of the strike team then observed the behavior of the tangos in the compound before spotting a draft of a routine, since the Russians were paire with two Houthi militants each while the lead militant and the Russian officer often walked with one other armed militant in tow. Shake also saw half of the militants always slept on a stool at night while the other half were standing guard.

Chapter 2

After a whole night worth of watch, the team saw the enemies were following the same routine since long before the commandos' arrival and had by now removed their night vision goggles not to be blinded by the very harsh sunlight and extreme heat of daytime in Yemen. Shake and her allies now knew the routine of their enemies and were going to strike at a moment's notice. AK, Shake and CK then motioned everyone to stand up and start slowly walking towards the compound before stopping at about 400 meters from their target and aiming their suppressed rifles at the guarding militants.

Suddenly, the militants' heads were popped out with their brains being splaterred all the way around by the 5.56 mm bullets fired by the M4A1 carbines used by the commandos, who then ran towards the compound and stacked at the door upon reaching the main gate of the compound.

Upon stacking at the gate, Shake took her knife from a pocket in her flak vest before removing the safety pin before one of the British Royal Marines opened the door and took out a militant by stabbing this guy in the kidney four times, killing the militant instantly. Shake and AK then snuck behind the Spetsnaz leader and the lead militant while the militiaman with them was killed by Ecks with a knife. AK then put his left hand on the lead militant's shoulder and right hand on the guy's mouth before violently snapping the militant's neck while Shake simultaneously put her left hand on the Spetsnaz officer's mouth and stabbed him in the throat before cutting the Russian's throat open, killing the guy instantly.

Teddy, Mix and Marky then slit three other Spetsnaz operators' throat while the other Royal Marines commandos strangled four militants to death before being joined by CK, Shake and AK, who had made their way to them by killing three other Spetsnaz men and six militants. Just then, a Royal Marine caught a militant and forced him to stay silent at knifepoint before Shake asked him where the hostages were in Arabic. The militant replied before getting his neck slit open.

"They put them in the smallest building in the compound." Shake informed everyone.

With that information, the team quickly reached the smallest building of the compound.

Just as the team reached another room, they stacked at the door and aimed their M4A1 carbines at the door. AK opened the door before he, Shake and CK shot the militants inside dead and turned around to face five distraught men. Shake and the others with her quickly looked at Shake's tablet before nodding and taking the freed captives with them. CK then got a radio message from his headset.

"Okay guys. Bad news. The LZ has been compromised and HMS Albion canceled the launching of helicopters. We'll have to walk through the desert." CK informed.

"Fuck. Means these fuckers must have been advised by the Russkies or the Iranians. Or even the Chinese." Shake correctly concluded.

With that, the hostages left the building by the rear door escorted by the commandos, who left only dead militants behind them before the sleeping militants could wake up. Taking their chance, the commandos and their protectees managed to leave the compound and get out in the desert. Just then, Mix took his compass and showed Southeast, to where the commando was to walk before reaching safety.

Chapter 3

Two hours after leaving the compound, the commandos and their protectees were walking in the desert when Shake, who was last in the escort, heard distant voices coming from behind.

She turned around and yelled to the others, "Contact! Six o'clock!"

Everyone turned around and put the protectees behind them before CK, AK and half of the team took a knee and shouldered their M4A1 carbines while Shake and the others stood and aimed their M4A1 rifles. Just as Shake thought, around twenty Houthi militants and ten Iranian specops came out at the horizon, wielding AK-47 rifles and RPK machine guns.

Just as the Iranians and their proxies appeared in their gunsights, the commandos opened fire. Shake fired her suppressed M4A1 carbine, killing two militants with two bullets in the chest and one in the head each before she hit one of the Iranian specops with two bullets to the forehead, killing that guy instantly.

AK hit two Iranian specops and three militants with several shots to the throat, killing them all, while Mix hit three militants with a headshot each. Their fellow US Marines, CK and his men also hit many more militants and the remaining Iranian specops dead with a hail of gunfire, forcing the last militants to fall back and run in disarray.

After ten more hours walking in the desert, the rescue team and their protectees finally found an elevated rocky ridge, where they finally took a pause to eat, drink and rest, which was a well-earned pause after hours walking into a huge strip of sand with bad guys chasing them and bound to kill the team.

Shake was also the one standing guard since everyone else was taking a nap to relieve themselves from a long and tiresome day hiking in a desolate and hostile country. As she stood guard, Shake saw two huge clouds of smoke through her binoculars. Looking closely, she realized these were pick-up trucks with ten Iranian Pasdaran soldiers, ten Russian Spetsnaz and even ten Chinese specops onboard alongside around forty Houthi militants.

"Shit! Russkies and their fucking friend won't let us breathe! They want these hostages bad!" Shake yelled to the others.

Everyone then stood up, retrieved their equipment and woke the protectees up before silently motioning them to follow the commandos. The freed civilians obeyed and followed the commandos while Shake planted some Claymore mines and rigged those mines to explode thanks to a laser-triggered detonator attached to each of them while Mix booby-trapped some M67 grenades and stuck them to rocks. Shake then ran up to her group just as the Russians, Chinese and Iranians arrived alongside the numerous Houthis.

Just as the US and British commandos, alongside the rescuees, left ridge, the Russians and their allies arrived and began combing the mountains for any signs of foreign forces and kill said foreign forces before catching the hostages and mock-execute them in a live feed. Two of the Russians and four Chinese specops then climbed up the hill before one of the Chinese touched a laser beam, causing the Claymore mine attached to it to explode. The schrapnels killed all of theses six enemies.

Ten Houthis and five Iranian Pasdaran soldiers were searching a crevice for any signs of the commandos when one of them stepped on the wire linking two M67 grenades, triggering the explosion and sent rock fragments flying all the way around, killing the five Iranians and nine of the Houthis. As another hostile team rushed at the location, one of the five Pasdaran soldiers in said team reported back the carnage to everyone else on his radio.

Suddenly, another explosion was heard before six Chinese soldiers and six Russians, alongside ten Houthis were blown out off the cliff by one of Mix's booby traps and fell to their death at the bottom of the ravine. Just then, two more explosions were heard, killing the remaining pursuers and giving more time for the commandos to run away.

As the explosive booby traps killed their pursuer, Shake smirked in mild satisfaction as the explosions warded their enemies off before running to her team. She knew her esteem in the team had by then increased since she proved her worth.

<u>Chapter 4</u>

In the middle of the desert, AK and CK stopped in the middle of nowhere, since night was falling and the group needed to rest for the duration of the cold freezing night. But the rescuees saw this break as a well-earned rest, since they barely had time to drink water while eating dried chocolate from the commandos' rations.

Marky and his spotter Ecks were standing guard and saw nothing but desert animals wandering around while two Royal Marines lit the fire, allowing everyone to have a source of heat for the night. But they also knew the fire could reveal their position, hence the guard shifts from the commandos.

Shake took some time to eat some food and drank some water before barely brushing her teeth. She was the first to take the first watch, since she was the least tired of the team.

Shake then began to take her turn before she spotted a dust of cloud. Looking through her binoculars, she saw it was just a pack of wolves hunting an oryx and killing it before eating the herbivore. Shake put her binoculars back in her pocket before taking her rifle back and began her watch, which was to last two hours.

As Shake and her team were taking a well-earned rest during the night, Shake listened to the conversation between the Americans and the British, which happened to be about her.

"Listen, she may be a rookie, but she's suited for our mission. So shut the fuck up!" AK said to Mark Dugan, Dan Finnegan, Carlos Miller and their Ukrainian bodyguards.

"I know. But I think it's irresponsible to bring a new member in your team." Dugan replied.

Just then, Teddy told, "Listen you civie fuck. Wasn't it for Shake, we would have fucked you up."

Miller then replied, "Yes, but you're not elegant at all. She shouldn't be wearing male clothing neither should she be wearing a shemagh."

Shake felt offended by those ungrateful civilians who only looked at her for her looks or clothing. She knew people tended to look at people based on their looks or clothing instead of competence, and she honestly felt at home with her father, stepmother and stepbrother, who had encouraged her to develop her competence instead of her looks and follow her dreams instead of theirs. And she now felt even more at home with the team, whose leader AK saw how talented of a leader and competent as a US Marine she was.

But she had time to further think about this, since Mix tapped her shoulder, signaling her it was time to take a nap. But Shake knew her nap would be a short one, since she was to relieve Mix afterwards.

The rest of the night went on and happened to be just as uneventful as the prolonged hike in the desert had been for the commandos.

But the team knew the hostages were of high value and that the Houthis, Iranians, Russians and Chinese would stop at nothing to recapture the freed aid workers while simultaneously kill the rescue team.

Chapter 5

The following day, the team left their improvised camp and were walking in the desert when Shake, who was dead last as usual, saw another cloud of dust in the distance. Looking through the scope of her M4A1 carbine, she realized it was a huge striped hyena eating a dead oryx after patiently waiting for the wolves to run off, knowing it couldn't stand a chance against a pack of twenty wolves.

Lowering her weapon, Shake ran towards her team and their protectees while the hyena watched them from afar. The hyena then resumed its meal before another fellow striped hyena joined the first one and shared the meal together.

Just then, a team of Russian Spetsnaz and Iranian Pasdaran joined by a whole company of Houthis arrived on scene. One of the pardaran soldiers saw footprints and had no trouble finding where the footprints were leading to.

Meanwhile, Shake, AK, Mix, Marky, Ecks, Teddy, CK and the Royal Marines were still boxing the rescued hostages while walking towards the sea, where they would be extracted by another team. But Shake had a bad feeling about the hike, since they had been running from the Houthis and their allies for two days now. Now was the third day and there was still nothing they could do except walk and hope they wouldn't stumble onto enemy forces.

Suddenly, a dust of cloud was seen in a distance before suddenly vanishing. Shake looked through the scope of her M4A1 carbine and realized it was hostile forces being forced to search the campfire previously used by the team and their protectees. Shake then took some M15 anti-tank mines, dug three holes into the sand and buried the mines before covering them with sand while her team kept walking. After burying her mines, Shake ran towards her team before catching up with them, knowing how inept the Russian army really was. She also knew the Chinese and Iranian commanders were just as inept as the Russian ones. Shake just hoped her mines would delay the pursuers long enough for the team to escape.

"Guys. Gotta buy us some time. Buried some mines over there." Shake informed her allies and the protectees.

CK then said, "Okay guys. Royal Marines, with me. AK, take your guys with you. We'll set a L-shaped ambush."

With that said, the British and American boots set up their ambush while hiding their protectees behind a large rock.

At the campfire site, the Iranian pasdaran soldiers, Russian spetsnaz and Houthi troops searching for footprints, as well as for remains of a meal, such as food packaging, toothpaste or toothpicks. Suddenly, one of the Houthi militants found footprints and just had to follow them to understand those they were pursuing were actually walking towards the sea, which meant their fleeing enemies hoped to evacuate via the Gulf of Aden.

The militant then said something to his friends before he and his friends armed their automatic rifles before boarding their pick-up trucks and driving away in the same direction of the footprints they found earlier. But what they didn't know was that they were about to roll into a deathtrap.

As the vehicles were coming closer and closer to the land mines Shake buried during the team's trip by foot, she and the rest of the team were lying in ambush 400 meters away from the minefield. Mark Dugan, Dan Finnegan, Carlos Miller and their Ukrainian bodyguards were cowering behind their rock as they saw their guardian angels preparing to fire their rifles at the attackers.

"Violence. Always violence. Why do they always have to resort to violence?" Mark Dugan asked aloud.

Finnegan then replied, "Because they have no elegance, no manners, no education and no bright mind. They're savages."

Miller replied, "Yes. Totally it. These guys are savages, they don't know chivalry or good manners in terms of education. The US Marine Corps shouldn't even exist."

Their bodyguards even nodded, because they were actually former policemen and not former soldiers. The protectees suddenly heard distant explosions and peaked over the rock to see burning pick-up trucks with several others stopped in their tracks. They also saw some dead bodies around the burning pick-up trucks while other men were standing in the open aiming their weapons everywhere.

As soon as the hostile forces aimed everywhere around, Shake and her team were the first to open fire, followed by CK and his men. Shake's bullets hit two Russians and one Iranian in the chest and the head, killing them instantly. AK shot dead three Russians and several Houthis dead with his M4A1 while Mix, Marky, Ecks and Teddy shot more Houthis dead with theirs. CK and his men killed several Iranian soldiers and Chinese specops dead with their M4A1 carbines before those Iranian, Russian, Chinese and Houthi troops could even fire.

While the British Royal Marines and Mix tossed smoke grenades to conceal their retreat, Shake and the

others retrieved their protectees
before Mix, Shake, CK and his men
joined them and withdrew with the
other of AK's men.

Chapter 6

After the successful ambush, the team did manage to escape alongside the protectees while the enemies were actually busy looking around for the team and the protectees while also aiming automatic weapons everywhere around the surrounding area, to no avail.

As the Iranian, Russian & Chinese soldiers and the Houthis militants were about to fire, they heard the lead Chinese soldier yell them not to fire and not to waste their ammunition, since they had wasted a lot of ammunition and had been forced to reload, even if their attackers had been forced to reload their weapons, too. But one of the Iranian soldiers counted the empty casings and remarked that their attackers left no magazine behind and concluded the latter must have used a pouch to store empty magazines.

Meanwhile, Shake and the rest of the team, alongside their protectees were still walking into the Yemeni desert when they suddenly heard something. Mix and Teddy looked through the scope of their M4A1 carbines and saw it was a patrolling Iranian Mi-17 helicopter, which was based in Yemen, flying towards them. Shake took her M72A7 LAW and extended it before aiming it at the tail rotor of the helicopter. She then fired it and waited for a few seconds until the rocket struck the tail rotor, causing the helicopter to crash while spinning uncontrollably before exploding upon hitting the ground.

The rescue party and the protectees then ran towards the wreckage, reaching it in minutes before discovering none of the Iranian crewmen of the helicopter survived the crash. Mark Dugan, Dan Finnegan, Carlos Miller and their Ukrainian bodyguards were horrified of the sight of the burning dead bodies inside the wreckage of the helicopter while the rescue team moved on. The protectees followed the team while Shake booby trapped the dead bodies with C4 charges before setting several charges on the wrecked Mi-17 helicopter itself.

Minutes after booby-trapping the crashed Iranian helicopter and its dead crew, Shake had caught up with the rest of the rescue team before hearing distant explosions. She understood it was her booby trap that had worked, killing and injuring many of the enemies who had arrived at the crash site.

The team and their protectees finally reached an abandoned oasis, where they afforded to take a rest. Mark Dugan, Dan Finnegan, Carlos Miller and their Ukrainian bodyguards set their tents, only for CK to tap their shoulder.

"Shouldn't go in your tents. And now, you're not giving orders anymore." He told the aid workers and their bodyguards.

The five of them then plunged into the lake of the oasis to take a proper bath while the rescue team barely set some sleeping mats further from the tents, which were overtly displaced further from the oasis. Shake herself took a bucket of water before washing herself with a few glasses of water and handing over hygiene duty to AK and Mix. Shake had just put her uniform and equipment back when she and the others saw the freed hostages coming over them and laying on the sleeping mats before the team slept onto the sand as Shake stood guard for half of the night, knowing their enemies could be looking forward to shooting at the campsite.

<u>Chapter 7</u>

The next morning, the team and their protectees had left the camp when Russian, Chinese, Iranian and Houthi forces reached it and discovered their targets were still pretty much alive and were way ahead of them. A few of the angry Houthis then aimed their Norinco Type 56 and AK-47 rifles at their fellow troops and shot these guys dead before continuing to pursue the foreigners who had manhandled them for such a long time.

In the HMS Albion, the USMC Major and the British Royal Marine Colonel were in the command center when a USMC Captain came inside. The officer then saluted his superiors before standing at ease.

"So. What's new?" the colonel asked.

The USMC Captain said, "Sir, we got some news. Satellite intelligence shows the second extraction point is lightly defended, since the tangos there are pursuing the team and the rescued hostages. But bad news is the rescue team will have to force their way through."

The British Royal Marine concluded, "Then we'll have to force our way through. Give order to a joint Royal Navy-US Marine direct action crews to prepare their CB90 patrol boats and fit them with heavy machine guns and automatic grenade launchers. Tell them to go for action tomorrow and meet the team at 18:00 hours sharp. Thanks you, captain."

The USMC captain and his superior saluted each other before the American captain left the command center.

A few seconds later, several Royal Navy sailors and US Marines loaded patrol boats with ammunition, explosives, fuel and medical kits, since they knew the rescue team could need some medical help if one of them was injured.

As the boat crews loaded their seaborne vehicles with supplies, several Royal Marines and US Marines boarded the boats and inspected the mounted Browning M2A1 heavy machine guns and the GAU-17 rotary-barrel machine guns mounted on the boats before loading them up with a mix of incendiary bullets, tracer rounds, explosive bullets and classic ball ammunition.

All of the boat crew knew their friends were there and probably needed help from the sea. And help would have to come in form of additional firepower should there be an encounter with Houthi forces and their allies.

In the meantime, the rescue team and their protectees were walking to escape their pursuers for the fourth day straight when Mix suddenly collapsed from sudden heat exhaustion. Shake took Mix's M4A1 carbine and carried it on her back before putting Mix over her shoulders to carry him to the extraction point, knowing full well how the Houthi forces would treat a captured American servicemember.

But Mark Dugan took a knife and tried to stab Shake, only to be shot at and wounded by CK, who helped Shake carrying Mix. An injured Mark Dugan, Dan Finnegan, Carlos Miller and their Ukrainian bodyguards had no other choice but to walk inbetween the commandos.

Chapter 8

After a few hours walking, the rescue team and the freed hostages finally reached a slightly elevated place, which actually was a hill featuring rocks and thick sand. The group then started climbing up a hill as Shake and CK still carried Mix before Teddy and Ecks hydrated their teammate, who slowly but surely regained consciousness. The commandos then had their protectees sit on the rocks while the commandos themselves also sat on the rocks as dusk settled in. The group then shared some rations before brushing their teeth and washing their faces before preparing to go to sleep.

Shake, glad that her teammate had gotten better, smirked at the team and their allies as they all drank some water from their hydration packs while the freed aid workers and their bodyguards drank some water before taking a nap.

Shake then said, "Guys. Have you ever seen a sunset in the desert? I mean, outside of Camp Pendleton, where we were trained?"

"No. Gotta admit it's really pretty over there." Mix answered.

AK, CK, Teddy, Ecks, Marky and the Royal Marines all laughed before taking some time to rest as Mix and Shake began their guard duty for the incoming night of night watch shifts.

After nightfall, Shake was keeping her watch when she suddenly saw something in the distant desert. Looking through her night-vision goggles, she realized the something she saw was actually a pack of oryxes being chased by striped hyenas. Shake then saw the weakest oryx of the pack tripping and getting mauled to death by the hyenas, which then proceeded to devour the herbivore.

"Such is the nature of life. We hunt, we kill and eat. Or we get killed and eaten." Shake muttered.

AK and the others heard Shake muttering, but knew it was one of her mannerisms when Shake wanted to cope with the horrors of war. They all had to cope with war before so it wasn't a surprise that Shake muttered, since she had her psychological defence mechanism to deal with the psychological aftermath of war.

Despite Shake being a rookie in the team, she was a fast learner since she now knew everything a US Recon Marine needed to know about modern warfare and combat, going as far as being the brains of the group, since AK ofter relied on her to scout ahead of them when they were in training and Shake had proven a remarkable asset for the team.

As one of the British Royal Marine was sitting on a rock, he spotted a camel spider and took his Glock 17 pistol before killing the spider with it while Shake killed a scorpion with her SIG-Sauer M18 pistol. Needless to say, the rest of the team woke up before falling back asleep.

Shake then stood watch for the first half of the night alongside Mix before the two of them, as well as the two British Royal Marines who were with them, were relieved before going to sleep for the rest of the night, knowing they needed every bit of rest, even if they were trained to resist sleep deprivation and lack of rest since boot camp.

"Good night guys." Shake said.

The others replied, "Good night, Shake."

"Let's fucking hope we can make it tomorrow. We've been walking for four fucking days straight with very few rest," said Shake. "Not to mention our fucking protectees aren't very cooperative."

"True. If we can, then we'll steal a truck before driving to the sea," a Royal Marine told. "As for our guests, then we'll release them when we're out of that country."

"Totally agree." AK replied. "I do know these guys don't like us, but I don't give a fuck about this. I won't give a fuck if they thank us or not. But I'll do the job. Even over my fucking life."

They all agreed they had a job to do and a mission to accomplish. Even if they didn't like their protectees' complaints and temper tantrums. These US Marines and their British counterparts had to deal with very hot daytime, extremely cold nights and the limited supplies they had in addition to dealing with whiny protectees.

Chapter 9

On the next day, at dawn's early light, the team decided to do everything it could to get a vehicle and drive towards the secondary extraction point. So Shake hatched a dangerous but audacious plan to get everyone out of Yemen when Mix suddenly heard something on his headset.

"Folks, bad news. The HMS Albion sent four armed boats to extract us at a beach six klicks east of the port of Aden. But we gotta be quick, since they'll meet us at 18:00 hours sharp." Mix told

"Alright, guys. Here's the plan. Two of CK's men will pretend to be injured Spetsnaz operators while we hide nearby. If a truck stops, we hold its owners at gunpoint, steal the truck and embark our protectees inside before getting the fuck outta here." Shake suggested after hearing Mix's report.

The others nodded at the idea, since they knew it was the only way to get out of Yemen fast, since they needed to meet the extraction force right on time. So two of CK's men ditched their M4A1 carbine, which were promptly taken by AK and Teddy before Shake and the others laid into a ditch from where they could ambush any incoming vehicle.

As soon as the two British Royal Marines laid on the road, the others were in the ditch, from where they spotted a cloud of smoke coming from the trail of dirt.

Shake and the others waited for the mysterious vehicle to come across the notionally wounded men who would be used as a distraction for the passengers of said vehicle before the team hijacked it.

Meanwhile at sea, the extraction team was riding in their

CB90 boats when their commander took his radio and turned it on.

"Okay everyone. Prepare your weapons. We're going in." he said.

With that, everyone loaded and armed their weapons while the crews armed the machine guns by chambering a round inside before gripping the Browning M2A1s and GAU-17s, ready for action.

All of the boat guys hoped they would arrive just in time to extract the rescue team and their protectees before the Houthis surrounded and exterminated them. They also knew if the Houthis didn't kill their friends, the Houthis' advisors would.

After fifteen minutes waiting for the vehicle to stop, the mysterious vehicle finally stopped after its driver saw the two "injured" men on the road. Just then, Shake and the others bursted out of the ditch and pointed their weapons at the two men from the vehicle. And the vehicle happened to be a Zil 131 truck, like those used in Vietnam on the Ho Chi Minh trail. But that truck was painted in plain yellow with a red stripe on the driver's cabin, marking it as a civilian truck.

Shake instructed the men in Arabic not to make any foolish move, or else she would kill them. While the two men stood still, the two Royal Marines stood up, took their rifles back and put the rescuees in the back of the truck before CK and his remaining men went with the protectees followed by Mix, AK, Teddy, Ecks and Marky. Shake being the best driver, she went for the driver's wheel and started the engine before driving off, leaving the two Yemenis with nothing but food and water.

Just as Shake drove far away from the two men, Mix took his radio and reported, "Albion, this Savior. We got the package. I repeat, we got the package. Heading to the secondary extraction zone now. Over."

The commander on the HMS Albion replied, "Savior, this is Albion. Solid copy. Remember to meet the extraction team at five klicks away from Aden. Out."

With that done, Mix and the others sat with their protectees while also remaining ready to return fire in case of an attack while Shake drove the truck at full speed.

Stevie "Shake" Randall was just a rookie on her first mission, but she was by now a far cry from the innocent girl she had been before joining the US Marines, since she had killed several enemies, taken the initiative before the team leader did and even stolen a truck after devising a plan to get out of a hostile country. Thus proving she had adapted, improvised and overcome a difficult situation as was expected from US Recon Marines.

Chapter 10

As soon as Shake came across a checkpoint of rebel Yemeni troops, she stopped the truck and lowered the glass, pretending she was just a woman helping her family out. When the rebel soldier asked her if she was a peasant, Shake dexterously manipulated him into believing her while the other rebel soldiers were searching the rear part of the truck. Shake was, however covertly reaching for her concealed SIG-Sauer M18 pistol while CK and two of his men took their Glock 17 pistols to take on the guards at the checkpoint.

Suddenly, as the two rebels searched the rear of the Zil 131 truck, they opened the tarpaulin at the back of the truck, discovering the fugitive. But before they could even yell a thing, CK put a hole in the first rebel soldier's head while his two men shot the second one dead with their pistols. Mix fired his

SIG-Sauer M18 pistol through the tarpaulin, killing the third checkpoint guard while Shake simultaneously revealed her pistol and swiftly pointed it at the lead guard's head before shooting him dead with a headshot. Once the guards were dealt with, Shake pressed accelerator and drove off at full speed, knowing they had compromised themselves by killing those guards, since one of them had time to radio for help.

In the meantime, the extraction team were coming closer and closer to the extraction point when they all armed their machine guns while the passengers put their shemagh on their face to prepare for the meeting with their friends, knowing these friends could need some help.

"Okay, guys. Let's do it. Bring our friends and the package back home." One of the commandos announced.

With that, they all prepared to go get their friends out of trouble.

After driving for nearly an hour off the road, Shake looked at the rearview mirror of the truck and saw several clouds of dust appearing behind the stolen Zil 131 truck.

"Guys. Got company. Pick-up trucks with DShKs plus militants toting FALs and AK-47s." Shake announced.

"Fuck! Let's point our weapons at the rear!" AK yelled.

Upon hearing AK's order, CK and his men pointed their weapons at the back of their truck while AK and his team protected the freed hostages, knowing they would have to give their life for the well-being of their protectees if needed.

As Shake was driving, she suddenly heard a bullet hit the armor panels on the truck and understood the pursuers must have opened fire on the Zil 131. She then suddenly heard gunfire coming from the back of the truck and understood it must be her allies firing back.

And CK and his men were indeed firing back at the pursuing pick-up trucks, trying their best to keep the militants in the trucks at bay. But the British Royal Marines were just as well-trained as their American counterparts. Three of CK's bullets hit the gunner of the first truck, killing that guy and sending him overboard while seven other bullets fired by two of his men killed the co-driver and one of the AK-47-armed militants in the back of the truck. The last three of CK's teammates killed four militants in the back of the second pursuing truck, including the driver, causing that pick-up truck to veer off course and crash into a large rock, sending the passenger and gunner flying over a short distance before they were killed when their head hit that rock.

In the third truck, another five militants plus the driver were killed by the British Royal Marines' bullets which hit them and caused their pick-up truck to crash into a large rock.

Shake then rolled over a small boulder, sending the Zil 131 truck airborne for a small bit, before it landed back on its wheels. Seeing the first pursuing truck had stopped, she knew it must have been hit either in the oil compartment of the engine block, or the two front wheels.

"Courtesy from the outside world!" Shake yelled.

The young female US Marine then drove at full speed towards the coast, where the extraction point was located. She indeed knew how to navigate through the featureless desert terrain due to her training at Recon School in Camp Pendleton.

Chapter 11

After several hours driving the stolen Zil 131 truck, Shake came into view of the secondary rendezvous point with the seaborne extraction team, which she knew was going to bring them back to the HMS Albion, where the rescue team would be finally enjoying some well-earned rest after days of running away from Houthi militants.

Upon seeing the extraction point, Shake pressed the gas pedal to roll full throttle towards said point on the beach when she suddenly saw more clouds of dust appearing behind her. Looking closely, she saw there were three pick-up trucks armed with PKM machine guns and carrying militants and Iranian soldiers carrying AK-47 rifles plus PKM machine guns.

"Fuck, more Houthis and Iranian soldiers coming. Right behind us!" she yelled.

AK then said, "Fuck, means they won't give up!"

With those words, Shake drove even further at the wheel of her truck while also dodging big rocks when she suddenly looked at the rearview mirror of the truck and saw one of the pursuing trucks exploding. Looking at the beach, Shake turned the wheel of the Zil 131 and drove onto the dirt road heading parallel of the beach while searching for the extraction team.

Suddenly, Shake spotted the armed CB90 gunboats with the members of the extraction team 500 meters to her left. She also saw the extraction team had brought Javelin missiles with them for bear against armored and non-armored targets in addition to using the machine guns mounted on the boats themselves.

Shake took a sharp turn and drove the truck towards the gunboats with the other Houthi vehicles chasing the Zil 131 truck while the rest of the rescue team fired their rifles towards the chasing militants, hitting some of them and causing these dead militants to fall out of the pick-up trucks.

After a while driving, Shake finally parked the Zil 131 truck at the extraction point, where everyone and the freed hostages disembarked the stolen truck before Shake booby-trapped it with some of her C4 charges before the hostages were pulled into the CB90 gunboats as the gunners opened fire with the Browning M2A1s and GAU-17s at the Houthi-Iranian-manned trucks.

One of the pick-up trucks was riddled with bullets that killed all of its occupants while the second one was hit by machine gun fire, riddling it with holes while simultaneously killing all of its passengers before both pick-up trucks exploded.

Shake then boarded one of the CB90 gunboats before hitting the detonator switch she had in her hand, destroying the stolen Zil 131 truck and destroying all evidence of American and British involvement in the Yemeni operation. The young female American Marine smirked upon seeing she wasn't that bad of a US Recon Marine after all.

Shortly after Shake blew the truck up, the CB90 gunboat crews turned the helm before speeding up towards the sea, where the HMS Albion was waiting for them. Turning around her team, Shake saw them smirking at her, letting her know they now fully accepted her as a member of the team.

Chapter 12

A week after the successful operation in Yemen, the freed hostages were now back to their families while Shake and the rest of the team were enjoying some free time in the HMS Albion. Shake and her team had taken a well-earned rest after days of sleep deprivation, sleeping in for several consecutive nights onboard the HMS Albion.

Therefore, Shake and the rest of her team were now better off and in very good shape since they now had a very complete eight hours of sleep per night after days of having to sleep for about just four or five hours of sleep per day, which meant they were tired to the point of collapsing once they were into the CB90s.

Shake and her team were in the second break room of the ship, while CK and his men were in the largest breaking room of the HMS Albion. Shake just wanted to have some sleep when she and the others of the team suddenly heard their phone beeping, prompting them to stand up and leave the break room before heading towards the armory, where they would retrieve their weapons and equipment.

At the briefing room, the now-fully armed team were alongside another team of British Royal Marines waiting for the officer in charge of the briefing. Said officer suddenly came into the room before Shake and the others stood at attention.

The briefing officer then said, "At ease. Now let's go on with the mission. The target is a cruise ship taken over by pirates who are armed with AK-47s, AK-74s and Uzi SMGs. Your mission consists in taking it back by either shooting or capturing every pirate onboard. But be careful, since they are led by an

Iranian Pasdaran colonel hell bent on unleashing hell on anyone who dares to face them. But don't worry. We will come at the target location, since we're at full speed. Any question?"

Seeing no one had any question, the briefing officer dismissed everyone before Shake and the rest of her team, as well as the British Royal Marines stood up and ran towards the EH101 Merlin helicopter, which was escorted by an AW159 Wildcat gunship whose gunner manned the pintle-mounted Browning M2A1 machine gun while the gunners of the EH101 Merlin manned the Minigun M134 mounted onto the windows for self-protection.

Meanwhile, at the bridge of the civilian ship, three pirates armed with AK-74s were standing guard when two men armed with Uzi machine guns came inside. One of them was none other than the Iranian colonel serving as an advisor to the pirates who had hijacked the ship.

"Everyone is gathered in the main dining rooms. As well as the main hallway." A pirate said.

One of the Iranian colonel replied, "Got it. Now stand guard and no one comes in or out without our direct order. Got it?"

One of the AK-74-armed individuals answered, "Got it."

As soon as the Uzi-carrying guys minus the Iranian colonel left the bridge, several gunmen carrying AK-47 rifles over their back tossed dead security contractors overboard into the sea before going back into the ship itself while laughing. The pirates not only hoped to get a huge profit but also hoped to get some political relevance since these pirates weren't the average type. They were actually mercenaries hired by Iran to disrupt free trade and trigger security issues in the Indian Ocean.

Chapter 13

After a few minutes flying into towards the target, the AW159 Wildcat began circling around before the gunner opened fire with the Browning M2A1 at the ship, forcing the pirates and their Iranian advisor to take cover and lie on the ground, thus allowing the EH101 Merlin to fly to the cruise ship and hover over the upper deck. Just as the Merlin helicopter began hovering over the target, Shake and a Royal Marine tossed a rope from each side of the big bird before sliding down the ropes.

Once on the deck, Shake and the Britishman aimed their M4A1 carbine while taking a defensive position to cover the others, who also slid down the ropes and took protective positions before the British commander and AK motioned the gunners to cut the rope, which was done since ropes were considered as expendable equipment.

Once everyone was set, AK and his British counterpart motioned everyone to split in duets to cover a wider area on the ship. And this strategy proved effective, especially as the helicopters flew away to refuel and rearm while the team would fight for the ship.

Just as Shake was joined by a British Royal Marine, she and the guy carefully went to the upper deck. Just as the duet arrived at the bottom of a stairwell, they met two mercenaries and pointed their M4A1 carbines at them before firing, killing those mercs dead with several shots to the chest before proceeding upstairs.

Simulataneously, AK and the British team leader were searching the lower deck when they stumbled on four mercenaries whom the duet immediately shot dead with their suppressed M4A1 carbines before keeping searching the area as Ecks and a British Royal Marine kept searching the area.

Suddenly, Ecks and his British comrade stumbled upon four patrolling mercenaries and shot the quartet dead with several shots to each of the mercenaries' chest before proceeding with the search of the ship after kicking the dead mercs' guns out of their hands.

The other teams led by Marky, Mix and Teddy swept the lower deck and shot the other mercenaries dead before converging to the inside of the ship while Shake and the Briton with her proceeded to the bridge. The rest of the joint team then proceeded to clean the corridors for any remaining hostile while watching each other's six o'clock and going in smoothly. Shake and the others indeed knew slow was smooth and smooth was fast, meaning it was better to proceed step by step and adapt to a changing environment rather than rush in the middle of nowhere.

Meanwhile, in the Command Information Center or CIC of the HMS Albion, the commanders of the joint US-British task force were watching a screen featuring a live feed by a MQ-9 Reaper UAV which was flying over the target while scanning the area around the hijacked cruise ship to spot any targets coming for the ship.

Both the two officers hoped the operation would go without too many problems while simultaneously knowing no plan could survive contact with the enemy. Especially if said plan had been set by officers who had little intel at worst and partial intel at best. They both hoped their troops would accomplish their mission with minimal losses.

<u>Chapter 14</u>

As the MQ-9 Reaper was circling around the target, Shake and a British Royal Marine arrived at the bridge, where the Iranian colonel and the lead mercenary fired their Uzis at the two Western servicemembers, narrowly missing Shake and the Brit who took cover behind the iron frame of the ship.

As Shake motioned the British Royal Marine to stack behind her, the Iranian colonel shouted, "You want to get me? Come there, American slut!"

Shake replied, "Fuck you! I'll get you anyway! Cause I'm not a fucking slut, neither a fucking patient girl!"

The female US Marine then took a stun grenade from her jacket and removed the safety pin before flicking the safety lever off with her thumb while the British Royal Marine took another stun grenade and removed the safety mechanism away with his fingers. Three seconds later, the duet tossed their stun grenades at the two hijackers, who had no time to react before the grenades went off, blinding both the Iranian colonel and the lead mercenary. Shake and the British Royal Marine then bursted out of cover and fired their suppressed M4A1 carbines at the two hostiles. Shake hit the Iranian colonel five times in the chest, killing him instantly, while the Brit hit the lead mercenary six times in the chest and two times in the head, killing the merc before Shake and the British servicemember picked the Uzis up, unloaded these guns and put them on the command console.

Suddenly, Shake heard a message from AK in her headset, "Everyone, move to the upper floor. Most of the mercs and hostages are gathered at the main hall."

With that, the American and British servicemembers moved to upper floor above the main hall by foot.

Shake knowing they would meet the others there before using CS gas, she put her M50 gas mask on her face to protect her lungs from the effects of CS gas. Shake had indeed been trained to handle the effects of CS gas during boot camp in a gas chamber which was designed to force recruits to keep their mask for thirty minutes straight before vacating the room.

After a few minutes walking, Shake and her British colleague joined the rest of their team before AK and the British team leader motioned them to prepare CS gas grenades for use. Shake took one of her M7 CS grenades and removing the safety pin and lever with her thumb before tossing the grenade as did Teddy and Ecks. The CS gas affected the hostages and the mercenaries alike while the team, including Shake, set their firing positions and fired their M4A1 carbines at the mercenaries, killing them with shots to the chest or the head, given that the team had been trained to fight in adverse conditions, any place, and any time.

As soon as Mix and Marky turned the ventilators on, the gas began to dissipate, revealing coughing and scared civilians as the team ran down the stairs before arriving at the main hall. Shake the revealed some more special abilities, shaped by intense training.

"Stay on the ground! Restez à terre! Bleiben sie auf den Boden, bitte!" Shake repeatedly yelled through her gas mask as she and the others made their way pointing their M4A1 carbines at everyone.

As the hostages remained on the ground, Shake spotted four mercenaries and pointed her M4A1 carbine at them before firing, soon joined by three British Royal Marines. The gunshots hit the mercenaries several times in the chest and the head, killing them instantly before these bad guys could fire their Kalashnikov variants.

Shake and the others then saw surrendering mercenaries, who threw their weapons on the ground and rose their hands in the air before kneeling down, thus ensuring the mission's success.

Shake then said, "Albion, this is Rapier. Target secure. Call the US Navy and their French friends for reinforcements and escort. Over."

"This is Albion. Solid copy. Out." The commander in the CIC of the HMS Albion replied.

<u>Chapter 15</u>

After the US Navy and French Navy secured the cruise ship after answering to the radio call for reinforcements from the HMS Albion, Shake and the rest of Rapier team took a well-earned rest aboard the HMS Albion after they handed the security of the cruise ship over to the US Navy SEALs and the French Commandos Marine, who were now going to take the ship to its actual destination.

Shake then said, "Guys, I bet we'll get another mission for the next three months. And said mission will probably take place in Somalia."

Mix replied, "I take the bet."

Marky then said, "Ain't no fucking boy scout in the team. Cause we're Recon Marines after all. And Shake's no fucking girl scout after all."

The team laughed before AK came into the room and motioned everyone to come into the briefing room. Shake, Teddy, Ecks, Marky and Mix got off their bunks and put their boonie cover on their head before walking to the briefing room alongside their team leader, who also had a boonie cover on his head like the rest of the team, since leaders are to show the example to their subordinates.

After siting down onto chairs at the briefing room, Shake and the rest of the team found themselves alongside another team of British Royal Marines before an officer came into the room, prompting the assault team to stand at attention.

The officer then rose his hand before the team sat in their chairs before saying, "Okay. Today's mission consists in raiding a hideout in Somalia. Because we've tracked the mercenaries to where they had met and pinpointed an old encampment in Somalia, where they are trained and advised by four Iranian Pasdaran officers who also supply them with automatic military-grade weapons such as Kalashnikov rifles, Uzis, G3s, QBZ rifles and RPGs. Needless to say, this camp is probably heavily guarded, so your mission is to snipe the Iranian advisors and the mercenary leaders. As for the extraction, you will be exfilled at the beach southeast of your sniping position."

Shake and the rest of the assault team saw the mugshots of the Iranian Pasdaran advisors and were also handed other mugshot pictures to help them identify their targets.

After the briefing, the team headed for the armory, where Shake took a Barrett M107 rifle, as did two British Royal Marines and Marky, while the others took their M4A1 carbines for the mission, knowing they would have to be extremely patient since it was an assassination mission.

Shake knew the US Marines would be a tough task, but she also knew she would lose her innocence and idealism, unlike her stepbrother who was still a naïve and idealistic boy scout back in the States. But Shake, whose real name was Stevie Randall, wasn't an idealistic girl anymore. She was a deadly US Recon Marine who was now willing to kill people to accomplish her mission, be her victims lone wolf terrorists or drug cartel members.

Just as the team finished retrieving their weapons and equipment, they embarked on a British EH-101 Merlin helicopter escorted by an AW-159 gunship, both of which took off from the HMS Albion and flew towards Somalia, where the sniper team would establish a firing position on

the top of a hill 1,500 meters from
their target.

Chapter 16

After hours of flying, the team arrived at the landing zone, where they jumped off the birds and ran to a safe position before motioning the helicopters to fly away. The two birds then flew away and headed back for the HMS Albion, where the helicopters would refuel and rearm before coming back for the team members at the coast.

Once the helicopters had left the area, Shake and the rest of the team walked towards their observation post, four kilometers away from the landing zone. Said observation post was located on a hill not too far from the compound, which would allow the team to effectively see and pick out their targets.

But this walk wouldn't be easy since the team was lugging a total of four Barrett M107 rifles in addition to their M4A1 carbines, pistols and other military equipment including backpacks, body armor, boots and knives.

After hours walking in the scorching desert at dusk, the team arrived at night at their observation post, where they set their M107 rifles for the mission, knowing they could have to wait for the arrival of their targets for hours, if not for days or weeks straight. Hence the fact Shake and the rest of her team took some more rations and water for the whole duration of the mission.

The team then began patiently waiting all night long for their targets to come, knowing these targets wouldn't escape from their gunsights, since the team was determined to put an end to the Iranian-sponsored attacks against international shipping lanes once and for all.

After the whole night and morning waiting for their targets, Shake and the other members of her team were tired since they had little time for a proper sleep, in addition to having to rest in the dirt and rocks of the desert. The young female US Recon Marine was now hunched over the Barrett M107 she took from the armory alongside Marky and two British Royal Marines when she suddenly spotted the four Iranian officers, a Major and three Captains.

Shake then said, "Eyes on target, eyes on target."

Ecks had put his binoculars on and told her, "You should pick the highest-ranking Iranian officer."

Shake set her sights on the Iranian major while the others set their scope on the other three Iranian Pasdaran officers.

Ecks then said, "Okay. Target distance 1,500 meters."

Shake then set her scope and replied, "1,500 meters. Good."

Ecks replied, "Right. Wind, North to South. Two klicks an hour."

Shake aimed her M107 at the right so that the bullet would be deported to the left side of the shooters. "Got it." She signaled.

Ecks said, "Nice. Add one for Coriolis force."

Shake aimed a little bit sideways before saying, "I'm good."

Ecks announced "Add one for the weather conditions."

Shake then set her rifle scope accordingly before she heard Ecks tell her, "Fire when ready."

Just as they finished setting their sniper rifles onto the targets, Shake and the other snipers flicked the safety off, chambered a round and fired their Barrett M107 rifle. A few seconds later, Shake saw the Iranian Islamic Revolution Guard Corps advisors getting hit by the powerful .50 caliber rounds. Shake's target got hit in the head, turning it into a messy mix of brains, blood and bone fragments with only the tongue remaining. The other Iranian officers were hit in the chest, boring a huge hole into their torso and briefly sending them airborne, killing these guys instantly.

After hitting their targets, Shake and the others took their Barrett M107 rifles and sensitive equipment before they moved away from the observation post, mission accomplished. Shake and her team moved alongside their British allies to a dirt road, where they managed to hijack a truck that arrived at the same time before quickly driving towards the extraction point.

During the drive, Shake stroked some dust off her face and clothing before quickly cleaning her M107 rifle and M4A1 carbine before

looking at the horizon, knowing
other missions would follow.

<u>Chapter 17</u>

A few hours after hijacking the truck, the team arrived at the extraction point, where they spotted the EH-101 Merlin waiting on the ground with its engines running while the AW-159 Wildcat was circling around in the sky to provide cover with its .50-caliber Browning M2A1 machine gun.

As Shake was the last to arrive at the landing zone, she and three British Royal Marines turned around to provide cover alongside the SBS operators who had already disembarked the Merlin helicopter while the rest of the strike team boarded the Merlin transport helicopter.

As he went past her, AK tapped Shake's shoulder, letting her know it was her turn. Shake and the others boarded the EH-101 before the SBS operatives followed them and closed the side doors of the helicopter. The pilot then took off and flew the helicopter back to the HMS Albion, followed by the AW-159 gunship.

Inside the EH-101 Merlin, Shake was taking a nap, as did the rest of the team while the SBS operatives were reporting the mission accomplished code, which was "Pizza eaten." Needless to say, high command knew the mission had been accomplished without trouble.

Shake was then woken up by AK, who leaned towards her as soon as she was awake.

"I'll leave the team alongside Mix to be transferred as Recon instructor at Pendleton while Mix will be transferred at Lejeune as survival instructor." AK informed her.

Mix, who also woke up, said, "AK's right. We leave you in charge of the team."

Shake smiled, knowing they were fully trusting her despite her being the rookie of the team. But looking around her, Shake saw the rest of her team nodding as an affirmative answer, since they all knew she was the best suited among them to get a promotion and become their team leader.

<u>Epilogue</u>

A single year after her mission in Somalia, Stevie Randall who by now went by "Shake", had been promoted to Corporal, leaving her in charge of a US Marine Recon team. All of her teammates, except Marky and Ecks, had been transferred to serve as instructors.

Just then, three rookies arrived and asked for Stevie Randall. Shake stood up from her bunk and walked towards the trio of rookies, surprising them since they didn't expect Shake to be a woman. They were even more surprised to see a face in her twenties as a team leader.

"Name's Shake. One rule: you're no fucking use to me dead." Shake announced them.

One of the rookies asked, "What was that pep-talk about?"

Marky said, "Want some fucking inspiration, Marine? Read a fucking poem."

That said, the three rookies, named Matt "Rye" Ryan, Eddie "Duke" Park and Raymond "Red" Fitzgerald, went for their bunks where they sat and put their duffle bags before taking a short nap.